MW00981308

To my wife Robyn,
who not only encouraged me to publish this story,
but was also the inspiration behind it.

The Reading Promise

Copyright © 2014 by Troy Kent

All rights reserved. No part of this publication may be reproduced or transmitted in any form or by any means, electronic or mechanical, including photocopy, recording, or any information storage and retrieval system, without permission in writing from the publisher.

Requests for permission to excerpt or make copies of any part of the work should be submitted online at info@mascotbooks.com or mailed to Mascot Books, 560 Herndon Parkway #120, Herndon, VA 20170.

PRT0514A

Printed in the United States

Library of Congress Control Number: 2014935773

ISBN-13: 9781620864043
ISBN-10: 1620864045

www.mascotbooks.com

The
Reading
Promise

Troy Kent

Illustrated by
Elisa Moriconi

Katherine became a mother for the first time. She named her baby boy Daniel. She was very happy that she had a baby, but she was also very scared. Katherine was scared because she had never been a mother before, so she wasn't sure what to do. There were a lot of things she didn't know, but she knew that she wanted to be a good mother.

Katherine didn't have much money though. She used all the money she had to buy
food and clothes for herself and her new baby. Sometimes Katherine even had to
buy medicine when Daniel was sick. She always thought of her baby first. Katherine
was a good mother even if she didn't know it.

One day Katherine took Daniel for a walk in his hand-me-down stroller.
As they walked down Main Street she saw a lot of other mothers with
their babies. Many of those mothers were buying fancy clothes and
expensive toys for their babies. Katherine even saw some mothers
taking their small children to the movies. Seeing how many things she
couldn't do for her little boy made her sad.

But she wasn't sad for long! When Katherine and Daniel turned onto Oak Street they came face-to-face with the Public Library, which gave her an idea. Reading to Daniel every night would be very special, and it wouldn't cost any money. So Katherine leaned over and whispered in his ear:

The day you were born, I loved you a lot.
So I'm making a promise, here on the spot.
My promise to you goes something like this:
I'll read to you every night, and end with a kiss.

So Katherine went into the library, got herself a library card, and signed out their very first book. She was very excited about this and couldn't wait to read Daniel the book, but before she could read it she had to feed him supper and bathe him.

After that, Katherine put him in a clean diaper and pajamas.
Then she cuddled Daniel in her arms and read.
When she finished the story she said:

> *The day you were born, I loved you a lot.*
> *So I'm making a promise, here on the spot.*
> *My promise to you goes something like this:*
> *I'll read to you every night, and end with a kiss.*

Katherine kissed Daniel on the cheek and laid him down
to sleep. She was very happy.

Katherine kept her promise
and she read to Daniel
every night. During the
day she would put him in
the stroller and they would
walk to the library to get
more books.

Sometimes they would sign out six books at a
time, especially if she thought it was going to
rain the next day. She was a very smart mother.

And every now and then, when Katherine did have some extra money, she'd buy Daniel a book. After a while he had quite a few books of his own on the shelf.

Well, like any other boy, Daniel continued to grow. In fact, Katherine thought he'd never stop growing! Before she knew it her baby was walking and talking...and talking and talking! Some days Katherine thought he'd never stop talking.

But every night, after she bathed him and put him to bed, Katherine read him a story. And each night, as Daniel was falling asleep, she whispered in his ear:

The day you were born, I loved you a lot,
So I made you a promise, back then on the spot.
The promise I made went something like this:
I'll read to you every night, and end with a kiss.

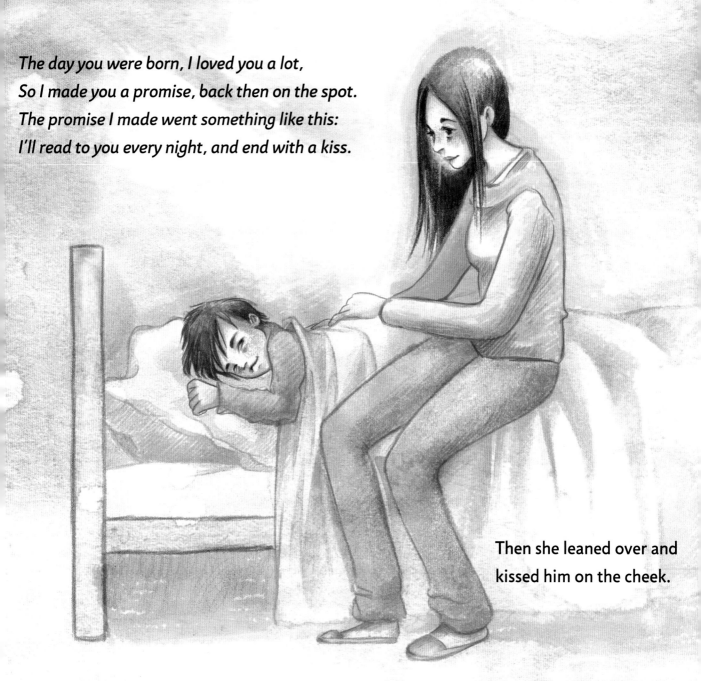

Then she leaned over and kissed him on the cheek.

Daniel kept getting older, and before Katherine knew it he wanted to read all on his own. Because she had read to him so many times, Daniel loved to read more than anything. She was a very smart mother. Soon, that boy could read anything! They read every night and talked about the things they read. Daniel had all kinds of questions and he learned all sorts of things. One night they read a book about dinosaurs that Daniel loved. So that weekend Katherine took him to the museum and he got to see the skeletons of real dinosaurs. Katherine loved taking him to the museum because it was another thing they could do together that didn't cost much money. Daniel couldn't believe how big the dinosaurs were! Katherine and Daniel came up with a lot of other things to do that didn't cost a lot of money, and these ideas always came from books. Once they read a book about a sea captain and they went fishing the next day with worms they dug up from their yard.

Another time they read a book about fireflies, so they stayed up a little later the next night to catch some in a jar. Then they read a book about trains, which Daniel also liked a lot, so Katherine took him to see a real one.

Daniel thought the train was really cool, especially
when he heard its whistle blow! They also read a book
about stars and galaxies, so a few nights later, when
the sky was really clear, they laid out a blanket and
looked up into the night sky. They were able to find the
Big Dipper and the Little Dipper!

Daniel was now in school and he was learning all kinds of new things. One night, when Katherine started to read him a story, he told her that he was too old for bedtime stories. This made her sad, but she always knew that day would come. Her little boy was growing into a man. So, like any other boy, he grew out of diapers and bedtime stories and started to do things that older kids do. But, no matter how old he got, Daniel often asked his mother to help him with his homework, and even if she was really tired Katherine always said yes. There were also many nights, when Daniel was fast asleep, that Katherine would tiptoe into his room and whisper to herself:

The day you were born, I loved you a lot,
So I made you a promise, back then on the spot.
The promise I made went something like this:
I'll read to you every night, and end with a kiss.

And even though she didn't read to him,
Katherine always snuck in another kiss.

Years went by and Daniel was all grown up. He finished school, went to college, and got a job. He got married, and one day his wife had her first baby. It was a girl.

Daniel was scared because he had never been a father before, so he wasn't sure what to do. There were a lot of things that he didn't know, but he knew that he wanted to be a good father. He also wanted to do something special for his little girl.

A short time later Katherine got very sick, so the doctor put her in the hospital. Daniel visited his mother every day, and while he was there he read her a story. She enjoyed it very much. One day, while Daniel was reading to her, Katherine closed her eyes and died quietly in her sleep. Daniel was very sad, but he finished the story anyway. He was sure she was still listening.

Daniel went home, and when he got there he went right to an old chest in his room. In it he found the first book that his mother had read to him. Katherine had given him his own copy when he was still a little boy, and it remained his favorite.

Daniel picked up his daughter and was just about to read it to her, but then he remembered that she hadn't had supper yet. So, he fed her supper, gave her a bath, and put her in a clean diaper and pajamas. Then, Daniel cuddled her in his arms and started to read that same old book.

As Daniel was reading the book he started to cry. He finally figured out what he could do that was special for his daughter. He realized that the time his mother spent reading to him was their very special time together, and no matter what happened in life he would always remember those times and those talks. Daniel leaned over and whispered in his baby's ear:

my first Book

The day you were born, I loved you a lot,
So I'm making a promise, here on the spot.
My promise to you goes something like this:
I'll read to you every night, and end with a kiss.

He was a very smart father.

About the Author

Troy Kent has been a high school English teacher for over two decades. He is a graduate of Acadia University in Wolfville, Nova Scotia. Troy currently resides in Long Sault, Ontario, with his wife Robyn and their five children. He is also the author of the whimsical children's book titled *Stinky Blinky*.

Our Reading Promise

I promise to read to _____ regularly,
no matter how busy I am.

_____

(Reader's Signature)

I promise to listen carefully, no matter how tired I am.

_____

(Listener's Signature)

_____

(Date)

Track your progress!

Date	Name of Book	Pages Read
_____	_____	_____
_____	_____	_____
_____	_____	_____
_____	_____	_____
_____	_____	_____
_____	_____	_____
_____	_____	_____
_____	_____	_____